Duets for Flute Students

by Fred Weber and Acton Ostling

LEVEL ONE (ELEMENTARY)

To The Teacher

Fifteen very easy duets for flute, with piano accompaniments. All are correlated with Part I of the Belwin "Student Instrumental Course" of instruction. All duets are carefully selected for their playability, musical value and appeal to students. They can be used for programs or contests as well as supplementary lesson and training material.

> *These duets can be played either with or without piano accompaniment. If played with piano, omit the small (cued) piano notes. If played without piano, play all notes -- both regular and cued.*

Contents

	Page		Page
Three Songs – *Traditional*	2	Forty-Five Minutes From Broadway – *Cohan*	9
Childhood Memories – *Traditional*	3	Yuletide – *Traditional*	10
Long, Long Ago – *Bayly*	4	Tiritomba – *Italian Folk Song*	11
Theme – *Mozart*	5	Sing Me A Song Of The South – *Casey*	12
Chopsticks – *Traditional*	6	Gypsy Love Song – *Herbert*	13
College March – *Elbel*	7	America The Beautiful March – *Ward*	14
I Love Little Willie – *Mountain Song*	8	Independence March – *Hall*	15
		Andantino – *Lemare*	16

The Belwin "STUDENT INSTRUMENTAL COURSE" - A course for individual and class instruction of LIKE instruments, at three levels, for all band instruments.

EACH BOOK IS COMPLETE IN ITSELF BUT ALL BOOKS ARE CORRELATED WITH EACH OTHER

METHOD
"The Flute Student"
For individual or Flute Class Instruction

ALTHOUGH EACH BOOK CAN BE USED SEPARATELY, IDEALLY, ALL SUPPLEMENTARY BOOKS SHOULD BE USED AS COMPANION BOOKS WITH THE METHOD

STUDIES AND MELODIOUS ETUDES
Supplementary scales, warm-up and technical drills, musicianship studies and melody-like studies.

TUNES FOR TECHNIC
Technical type melodies, variations, and "famous passages" from musical literature --- for the development of technical dexterity.

THE FLUTE SOLOIST
Interesting and playable graded easy solo arrangements of famous and well-liked melodies. Also contains 2 Duets, and 1 Trio. Easy piano accompaniments.

DUETS FOR STUDENTS
Easy duet arrangements of familiar melodies for early ensemble experience.
Available for: Flute
B♭ Clarinet
Alto Sax
B♭ Cornet
Trombone

Three Songs

Childhood Memories

Long, Long Ago

BAYLY

Theme

MOZART

Chopsticks

TRADITIONAL

College March

March tempo

ELBEL

I Love Little Willie

Moderato

Piano

MOUNTAIN SONG

(Play in absence of piano.)

Forty-Five Minutes From Broadway

COHAN

Yuletide

Tiritomba

Allegretto

ITALIAN FOLK SONG

Sing Me A Song Of The South

Moderato

CASEY

Gypsy Love Song

HERBERT

Tranquilly

America The Beautiful March

WARD

Independence March

HALL

Andantino

LEMARE